To my mother 1875–1928 – P. L. T.

For my mother – thank you – L. C.

Illustrated by
LAUREN CHILD

Mary Poppins

Written by
P. L. TRAVERS

HarperCollins *Children's Books*

Contents

Foreword

I FIRST DISCOVERED MARY POPPINS AS A CHILD WHEN I WAS TAKEN TO SEE THE 1964 *Disney film. It was the first time I had ever watched a film in a cinema. It was quite an occasion, and one of those outings so beloved that it has become part of my family history. The experience of watching Mary Poppins on the large screen: sliding up the banisters, pouring three differently coloured medicines from one single bottle and tidying a room with a snap of the fingers left me wondering . . . How was it done?*

But did I even want to know? *Was it more exciting to simply believe in the magic appearing before me? That indeed it* might *be possible to laugh so much that one would actually float up to the ceiling?*

For me, this is the art of good storytelling, whatever the medium. To create a fictional world so compelling that one wants to believe in it and almost *does. The Walt Disney film with its then state-of-the-art special effects perfectly captured the magic of the story. It was a beautifully composed adaptation of P. L. Travers's extraordinary book. A book that I sought out as soon as it dawned on me that Mary Poppins had a life beyond the screen.*

It has been such a pleasure to reread the original book I so loved as a child and have the chance to illustrate my favourite stories from it. Published in 1934, Mary Poppins *features twelve charming and peculiar episodes that tell the story of a remarkable nanny who alights at the Banks family's front door, blown in on the east wind. In fact, she is* hurled *at the front door by the east wind – there is nothing delicate about Mary Poppins. The seven chapters I chose to illustrate and include in this collection were the ones I found particularly thought-provoking and joyful – although all of them are extraordinarily imaginative simply because Travers had the most incredible mind.*

I was particularly struck by the chapter titled "John and Barbara's Story". It does not appear in the film adaptation, but in many ways to me is the most poignant of all. Central to the story is the notion that children can communicate with animals until they reach their first birthday. As soon as the child turns one, they forget absolutely everything, becoming the gurgling infant we always considered them to be. I was fascinated by this idea when I first read

Mary Poppins *as a child. It was such a wonderful yet melancholy thought – and I can't help wondering if Travers was reflecting upon how quickly the innocence and imagination of childhood is lost.*

I chose to set my illustrated edition in the 1930s, echoing the period in which it was first published. Many of the characters' costumes are based on clothing from that time, although – because we're never really sure where Mary comes from, or if she's even of this world – I dressed her in a more Edwardian style but with a contemporary twist.

Perhaps because she is someone known by so many, for so many years, it felt right to draw Mary in a traditional style. However, I have combined this with collage, using vivid patterns and colours throughout to lend a vibrancy to the artwork by including fabrics as wallpapers, floors, clothing and decoration. These help to bring a modernity perfectly suited to the story. I have created a tweed coat for Mary as it seemed fitting she would wear a traditional good quality, workaday fabric, but I also wanted it to have an elegant eccentricity. I happened to have a few fabric swatches from the outfitters Dashing Tweeds, which I thought would be perfect for her. The one I chose is a beautiful vivid yellow-and-black weave. If you saw it in real life, you would notice a reflective thread running through it so it appears to illuminate if a light is shone at it. It seemed to me to be exactly what Mary Poppins might wear as the perfect marriage of practicality and magic.

The real joy of Mary Poppins is that she is a timeless and enduring character – and one who has beguiled me since I first encountered her. It has been an honour to bring her to life in this way and to introduce her to new readers who I hope will stay equally as enchanted with her as I am.

Lauren Child

ONE

East Wind

IF YOU WANT TO FIND CHERRY TREE LANE ALL
you have to do is ask the Policeman at the crossroads.
He will push his helmet slightly to one side, scratch
his head thoughtfully, and then he will point his huge
finger and say:

"First to your right,
second to your left,
sharp right again,
and you're there.
Good morning."

And sure enough, if you follow his directions exactly, you *will* be there – right in the middle of Cherry Tree Lane, where the houses run down one side and the Park runs down the other and the cherry trees go dancing right down the middle.

If you are looking for Number Seventeen – and it is more than likely that you will be, for this book is all about that particular house – you will very soon find it. To begin with, it is the smallest house in the Lane. And besides that, it is the only one that is rather dilapidated and needs a coat of paint. But Mr Banks, who owns it, said to Mrs Banks that she could have either a nice, clean, comfortable house or four children. But not both, for he couldn't afford it.

And after Mrs Banks had given the matter some consideration she came to the conclusion that she would rather have Jane, who was the eldest, and Michael, who came next, and John and Barbara, who were Twins and came last of all. So it was settled, and that was how the Banks family came to live at Number Seventeen, with Mrs Brill to cook for them, and Ellen to lay the tables, and Robertson Ay to cut the lawn and clean the knives and polish the shoes and, as Mr Banks always said, "to waste his time and my money".

And, of course, besides these there was Katie Nanna,
who doesn't really deserve to
come into the book at all

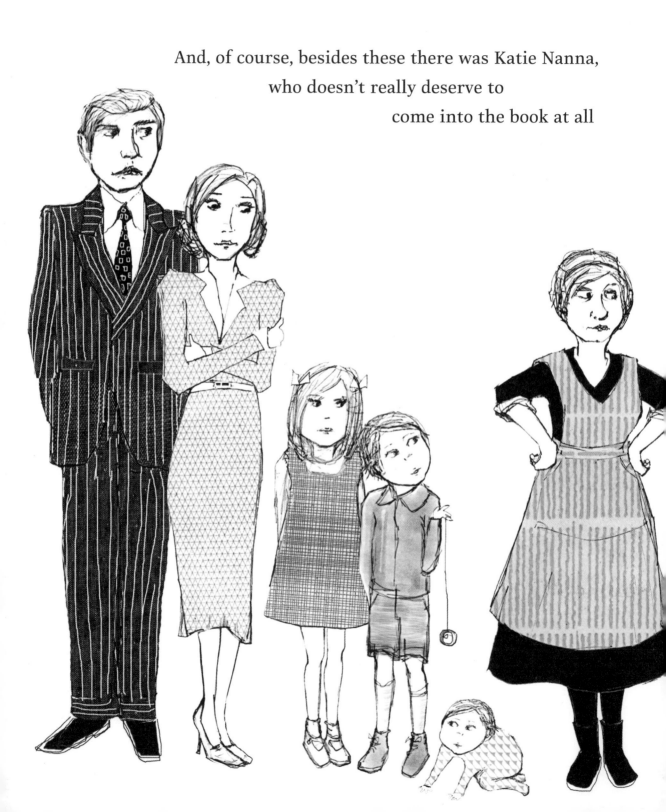

because, at the time I am speaking of,

she had just left

Number Seventeen.

"Without a by your leave or a word of warning. And what am I to do?" said Mrs Banks.

"Advertise, my dear," said Mr Banks, putting on his shoes. "And I wish Robertson Ay would go without a word of warning, for he has again polished one boot and left the other untouched. I shall look very lopsided."

"That," said Mrs Banks, "is not of the least importance. You haven't told me what I'm to do about Katie Nanna."

"I don't see how you can do anything about her since she has disappeared," replied Mr Banks. "But if it were me – I mean I – well, I should get somebody to put in the *Morning Paper* the news that Jane and Michael and John and Barbara Banks (to say nothing of their mother) require the best possible Nannie at the lowest possible wage and at once. Then I should wait and watch for the Nannies to queue up outside the front gate, and I should get very cross with them for holding up the traffic and making it necessary for me to give the Policeman a shilling for putting him to so much trouble. Now I must be off. Whew, it's as cold as the North Pole. Which way is the wind blowing?"

And as he said that, Mr Banks popped his head out of the window and looked down the Lane to Admiral Boom's house at the corner. This was the grandest house in the Lane, and the Lane was very proud of it because it was built exactly like a ship. There was a flagstaff in the garden, and on the roof was a gilt weathercock shaped like a telescope.

"Ha!" said Mr Banks, drawing in his head very quickly. "Admiral's telescope says East Wind. I thought as much. There is frost in my bones. I shall wear two overcoats." And he kissed his wife absentmindedly on one side of her nose and waved to the children and went away to the City.

Now, the City was a place where Mr Banks went every day – except Sundays, of course, and Bank Holidays – and while he was there he sat on a large chair in front of a large desk and made money. All day long he worked, cutting out pennies and shillings and half-crowns and threepenny-bits. And he brought them home with him in his little black bag. Sometimes he would give some to Jane and Michael for their money-boxes, and when he couldn't spare any he would say, "The Bank is broken," and they would know he hadn't made much money that day.

Well, Mr Banks went off with his black bag, and Mrs Banks went into the drawing room and sat there all day long writing letters to the papers and begging them to send some Nannies to her at once as she was waiting; and upstairs in the Nursery, Jane and Michael watched at the window and wondered who would come. They were glad Katie Nanna had gone, for they had never liked her. She was old and fat and smelt of barley-water. Anything, they thought, would be better than Katie Nanna – if not *much* better.

When the afternoon began to die away behind the Park, Mrs Brill and Ellen came to give them their supper and to bath the Twins. And after supper Jane and Michael sat at the window watching for Mr Banks to come home, and listening to

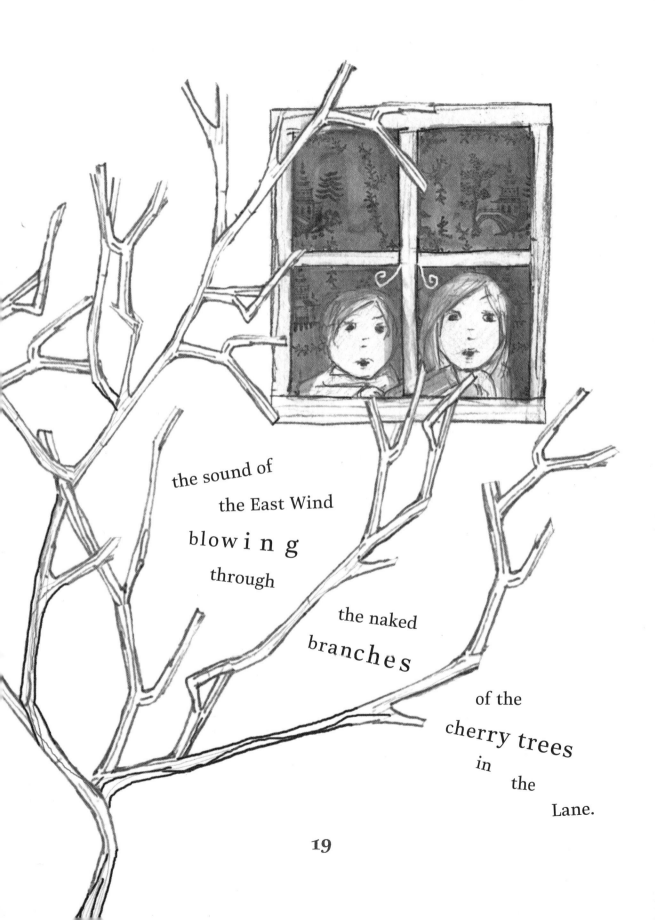

the sound of
the East Wind
blow i n g
through

the naked
branches

of the
cherry trees
in   the
Lane.

19

The trees themselves, turning and bending in the half light, looked as though they had gone mad and were dancing their roots out of the ground.

"There he is!" said Michael, pointing suddenly to a shape that banged heavily against the gate. Jane peered through the gathering darkness.

"That's not Daddy," she said. "It's somebody else."

Then the shape, tossed and bent under the wind, lifted the latch of the gate, and they could see that it belonged to a woman, who was holding her hat on with one hand and carrying a bag in the other. As they watched, Jane and Michael saw a curious thing happen. As soon as the shape was inside the gate the wind seemed to catch her up into the air and fling her at the house. It was as though it had flung her first at the gate, waited for her to open it, and then lifted and thrown her, bag and all, at the front door.

The watching children heard a terrific bang, and as she landed the whole house shook.

"How funny! I've never seen that happen before," said Michael.

"Let's go and see who it is!" said Jane, and taking Michael's arm she drew him away from the window, through the Nursery and out on to the landing. From there they always had a good view of anything that happened in the front hall.

Presently they saw their Mother coming out of the drawing room with a visitor following her. Jane and Michael could see that the newcomer had shiny black hair – "Rather like a wooden Dutch doll," whispered Jane. And that she was thin, with large feet and hands, and small, rather peering blue eyes.

"You'll find that they are very nice children," Mrs Banks was saying.

Michael's elbow gave a sharp dig at Jane's ribs.

"And that they give no trouble at all," continued Mrs Banks uncertainly, as if she herself didn't really believe what she was saying. They heard the visitor sniff as though *she* didn't either.

"Now, about references—" Mrs Banks went on.

"Oh, I make it a rule never to give references," said the other firmly. Mrs Banks stared.

"But I thought it was usual," she said. "I mean – I understood people always did."

"A very old-fashioned idea, to *my* mind," Jane and Michael heard the stern voice say. "*Very* old-fashioned. *Quite* out of date, as you might say."

Now, if there was one thing Mrs Banks did not like, it was to be thought old-fashioned. She just couldn't bear it. So she said quickly:

"Very well, then. We won't bother about them. I only asked, of course, in case *you* – er – required it. The Nursery is upstairs—" And she led the way towards the staircase, talking all the time, without stopping once. And because she was doing that Mrs Banks did not notice what was happening behind her, but Jane and Michael, watching from the top landing, had an excellent view of the extraordinary thing the visitor now did.

Certainly she followed Mrs Banks upstairs, but not in the usual way. With her large bag in her hands she slid gracefully *up* the banisters, and arrived at the landing at the same time as Mrs Banks. Such a thing, Jane and Michael knew, had never been done before. Down, of course, for they had often done it themselves. But up – never! They gazed curiously at the strange new visitor.

"Well, that's all settled, then." A sigh of relief came from the children's Mother.

"Quite. As long as *I'm* satisfied," said the other, wiping her nose with a large red and white bandanna handkerchief.

"Why, children," said Mrs Banks, noticing them suddenly, "what are you doing there? This is your new nurse, Mary Poppins. Jane, Michael, say how do you do! And these" – she waved her hand at the babies in their cots – "are the Twins."

Mary Poppins regarded them steadily, looking from one to the other as though she were making up her mind whether she liked them or not.

"Will we do?" said Michael.

"Michael, don't be naughty," said his Mother.

Mary Poppins continued to regard the four children searchingly. Then, with a long, loud sniff that seemed to indicate that she had made up her mind, she said:

"I'll take the position."

"For all the world," as Mrs Banks said to her husband later, "as though she were doing us a signal honour."

"Perhaps she is," said Mr Banks, putting his nose round the corner of the newspaper for a moment and then withdrawing it very quickly.

When their Mother had gone, Jane and Michael edged towards Mary Poppins, who stood, still as a post, with her hands folded in front of her.

"How did you come?" Jane asked. "It looked just as if the wind blew you here."

"It did," said Mary Poppins briefly. And she proceeded to unwind her muffler from her neck and to take off her hat, which she hung on one of the bedposts.

As it did not seem as though Mary Poppins was going to say any more – though she sniffed a great deal –

Jane, too, remained silent. But when she bent down to undo her bag, Michael could not restrain himself.

"What a funny bag!" he said, pinching it with his fingers.

"Carpet," said Mary Poppins, putting her key in the lock.

"To carry carpets in, you mean?"

"No. Made of."

"Oh," said Michael. "I see." But he didn't – quite.

By this time the bag was open, and Jane and Michael were more than surprised to find it was completely empty.

"Why," said Jane, "there's nothing in it!"

"What do you mean – nothing?" demanded Mary Poppins, drawing herself up and looking as though she had been insulted. "Nothing in it, did you say?"

And with that she took out from the empty bag a starched white apron and tied it round her waist. Next she unpacked a large cake of Sunlight Soap, a toothbrush, a packet of hairpins, a bottle of scent, a small folding armchair and a box of throat lozenges.

Jane and Michael stared.

"But I *saw*," whispered Michael. "I'm sure it was empty."

"Hush!" said Jane, as Mary Poppins took out a large bottle labelled "One Teaspoon to be Taken at Bedtime".

A spoon was attached to the neck of the bottle, and into this Mary Poppins poured a dark crimson fluid.

"Is that your medicine?" enquired Michael, looking very interested.

"No, yours," said Mary Poppins, holding out the spoon to him. Michael stared. He wrinkled up his nose. He began to protest.

"I don't want it. I don't need it. I won't!"

But Mary Poppins's eyes were fixed upon him, and Michael suddenly discovered that you could not look at Mary Poppins and disobey her. There was something strange and extraordinary about her – something that was frightening and at the same time most exciting. The spoon came nearer. He held his breath, shut his eyes and gulped. A delicious taste ran round his mouth. He turned his tongue in it. He swallowed, and a happy smile ran round his face.

"Strawberry ice," he said ecstatically. "More, more, more!"

But Mary Poppins, her face as stern as before, was pouring out a dose for Jane. It ran into the spoon, silvery, greeny, yellowy. Jane tasted it.

"Lime-juice cordial," she said, sliding her tongue deliciously over her lips.

But when she saw Mary Poppins moving towards the Twins with the bottle Jane rushed at her. "Oh, no – please. They're too young. It wouldn't be good for them. Please!"

Mary Poppins, however, took no notice, but with a warning, terrible glance at Jane, tipped the spoon towards John's mouth. He lapped at it eagerly,

and by the few drops that were spilt on his bib, Jane and Michael could tell that the substance in the spoon this time was milk.

Then Barbara had her share, and she gurgled and licked the spoon twice. Mary Poppins then poured out another dose and solemnly took it herself.

"Rum punch," she said, smacking her lips and corking the bottle.

Jane's eyes and Michael's popped with astonishment, but they were not given much time to wonder, for Mary Poppins, having put the miraculous bottle on the mantelpiece, turned to them.

"Now," she said,

"spit-spot into bed."

And she began to undress them. They noticed that whereas buttons and hooks had needed all sorts of coaxing from Katie Nanna, for Mary Poppins they flew apart almost at a look. In less than a minute they found themselves in bed and watching, by the dim light from the night-light, the rest of Mary Poppins's unpacking being performed.

From the carpet bag she took out seven flannel nightgowns, four cotton ones, a pair of boots, a set of dominoes, two bathing-caps and a postcard album. Last of all came a folding camp-bedstead with blankets and eiderdown complete, and this she set down between John's cot and Barbara's.

Jane and Michael sat hugging themselves and

watching. It was all so surprising that they could find nothing to say. But they knew, both of them, that something strange and wonderful had happened at Number Seventeen, Cherry Tree Lane.

Mary Poppins, slipping one of the flannel nightgowns over her head, began to undress underneath it as though it were a tent. Michael, charmed by this strange new arrival, unable to keep silent any longer, called to her.

"Mary Poppins," he cried, "you'll never leave us, will you?"

There was no reply from under the nightgown. Michael could not bear it.

"You won't leave us, will you?" he called anxiously.

Mary Poppins's head came out of the top of the nightgown. She looked very fierce.

"One word more from that direction," she said threateningly, "and I'll call the Policeman."

"I was only saying," began Michael, meekly, "that we hoped you wouldn't be going away soon—" He stopped, feeling very red and confused.

Mary Poppins stared from him to Jane in silence. Then she sniffed.

"I'll stay till the wind changes," she said shortly, and she blew out her candle and got into bed.

"That's all right," said Michael, half to himself and half to Jane. But Jane wasn't listening. She was thinking about all that had happened, and wondering . . .

And that is how Mary Poppins came to live at Number Seventeen, Cherry Tree Lane. And although they sometimes found themselves wishing for the quieter, more ordinary days when Katie Nanna ruled the household, everybody, on the whole, was glad of Mary Poppins's arrival. Mr Banks was glad because, as she arrived by herself and did not hold up the traffic, he had not had to tip the Policeman. Mrs Banks was glad because she was able to tell everybody that *her* children's nurse was so fashionable that she didn't believe in giving references. Mrs Brill and Ellen were glad because they could drink strong cups of tea all day in the kitchen and no longer needed to preside at

Nursery suppers. Robertson Ay was glad, too, because Mary Poppins had only one pair of shoes, and those she polished herself.

But nobody ever knew what Mary Poppins felt about it, for Mary Poppins never told anything . . .

The Day Out

TWO

The Day Out

"EVERY THIRD THURSDAY," SAID MRS BANKS. "Two till five."

Mary Poppins eyed her sternly. "The best people, ma'am," she said, "give every *second* Thursday, and one till six. And those I shall take or—" Mary Poppins paused, and Mrs Banks knew what the pause meant. It meant that if she didn't get what she wanted Mary Poppins would not stay.

"Very well, very well," said Mrs Banks hurriedly, though she wished Mary Poppins did not know so very much more about the best people than she did herself.

So Mary Poppins put on her white gloves and tucked her umbrella under her arm – not because it was raining but because it had such a beautiful handle that she couldn't possibly leave it at home. How could you leave your umbrella behind if it had a parrot's head for a handle? Besides, Mary Poppins was very vain and liked to look her best. Indeed, she was quite sure that she never looked anything else.

Jane waved to her from the Nursery window.

"Where are you going?" she called.

"Kindly close that window," replied Mary Poppins, and Jane's head hurriedly disappeared inside the Nursery.

Mary Poppins walked down the garden path and opened the gate. Once outside in the Lane, she set off walking very quickly as if she were afraid the afternoon would run away from her if she didn't keep up with it. At the corner she turned to the right and then to the left, nodded haughtily to the Policeman, who said it was a nice day, and by that time she felt that her Day Out had begun.

She stopped beside an empty motor car in order to put her hat straight with the help of the windscreen, in which it was reflected, then she smoothed down her frock and tucked her umbrella more securely under her arm so that the handle, or rather the parrot, could be seen by everybody. After these preparations she went forward to meet the Match Man.

Now, the Match Man had two professions. He not only sold matches like any ordinary match man, but he drew pavement pictures as well. He did these things turn-about according to the weather. If it was wet, he sold matches because the rain would have washed away his pictures if he had painted them. If it was fine, he was on his knees all day, making pictures in coloured chalks on the side-walks, and doing them so quickly that often you would find he had painted up one side of a street and down the other almost before you'd had time to come round the corner.

On this particular day, which was fine but cold, he was painting. He was in the act of adding a picture of two Bananas, an Apple, and a head of Queen Elizabeth to a long string of others, when Mary Poppins walked up to him, tiptoeing so as to surprise him.

"Hey!" called Mary Poppins softly.

He went on putting brown stripes on a banana and brown curls on Queen Elizabeth's head.

"Ahem!" said Mary Poppins, with a ladylike cough.

He turned with a start and saw her.

"Mary!" he cried, and you could tell by the way he cried it that Mary Poppins was a very important person in his life.

Mary Poppins looked down at her feet and rubbed the toe of one shoe along the pavement two or three times. Then she smiled at the shoe in such a way that the shoe knew quite well that the smile wasn't meant for it.

"It's my Day, Bert," she said. "Didn't you remember?" Bert was the Match Man's name – Herbert Alfred for Sundays.

44

"Of course I remembered, Mary," he said, "but—" and he stopped and looked sadly into his cap. It lay on the ground beside his last picture and there was tuppence in it. He picked it up and jingled the pennies.

"That all you got, Bert?" said Mary Poppins, and she said it so brightly you could hardly tell she was disappointed at all.

"That's the lot," he said. "Business is bad today. You'd think anybody'd be glad to pay to see that, wouldn't you?" And he nodded his head at Queen Elizabeth. "Well – that's how it is, Mary," he sighed. "Can't take you to tea today, I'm afraid."

Mary Poppins thought of the raspberry-jam cakes they always had on her Day Out, and she was just going to sigh, when she saw the Match Man's face. So, very cleverly, she turned the sigh into a smile – a good one with both ends turned up – and said:

"That's all right, Bert. Don't you mind. I'd much rather not go to tea. A stodgy meal, I call it – really."

And that, when you think how very much she liked raspberry-jam cakes, was rather nice of Mary Poppins.

The Match Man apparently thought so, too, for he took her white-gloved hand in his and squeezed it hard. Then together they walked down the row of pictures.

"Now, *there's* one you've never seen before!" said the Match Man proudly, pointing to a painting of a mountain covered with snow and its slopes simply littered

with grasshoppers sitting on gigantic roses.

This time Mary Poppins could indulge in a sigh without hurting his feelings.

"Oh, Bert," she said, "that's a fair treat!" And by the way she said it she made him feel that by rights the picture should have been in the Royal Academy, which is a large room where people hang the pictures they have painted. Everybody comes to see them, and when they have looked at them for a very long time, everybody says to everybody else: "The idea – my dear!"

The next picture Mary Poppins and the Match Man came to was even better. It was the country – all trees and grass and a little bit of blue sea in the distance, and something that looked like Margate in the background.

"My word!" said Mary Poppins admiringly, stooping so that she could see it better. "Why, Bert, whatever is the matter?"

For the Match Man had caught hold of her other hand now and was looking very excited.

"Mary," he said, "I got an idea! A real *idea*. Why don't we go there – right now – this very day? Both together, into the picture. Eh, Mary?"

And still holding her hands he drew her
right out of the street, away from the
iron railings and the lamp-posts,
into the very
middle of the picture.

Pff!

There they were,
right inside it!

How green it was there
and how quiet, and what soft
crisp grass under their feet!

They could hardly believe it was true, and yet here were green branches huskily rattling on their hats as they bent beneath them, and little coloured flowers curling round their shoes. They stared at each other, and each noticed that the other had changed. To Mary Poppins, the Match Man seemed to have bought himself an entirely new suit of clothes, for he was now wearing a striped coat and white flannel trousers and, best of all, a new straw hat. He looked unusually clean, as though he had been polished.

"Why, Bert, you look fine!" she cried in an admiring voice.

Bert could not say anything for a moment, for his mouth had fallen open and he was staring at her with round eyes. Then he gulped and said: "Golly!"

That was all. But he said it in such a way and stared so steadily and so delightedly at her that she took a little mirror out of her bag and looked at herself in it.

She, too, she discovered, had changed. Round her shoulders hung a cloak of lovely artificial silk with watery patterns all over it, and the tickling feeling at the back of her neck came, the mirror told her, from a long curly feather that swept down from the brim of her hat. Her best shoes had disappeared, and in their place were others much finer and with large diamond buckles shining upon them. She was still wearing the white gloves and carrying the umbrella.

"My goodness," said Mary Poppins, "I *am* having a Day Out!"

So, still admiring themselves and each other, they moved on together through the little wood, till presently they came upon a little open space filled with sunlight. And there on a green table was Afternoon Tea!

A pile of raspberry-jam cakes as high as Mary Poppins's waist stood in the centre, and beside it tea was boiling in a big brass urn. Best of all, there were two plates of whelks and two pins to pick them out with.

"Strike me pink!" said Mary Poppins. That was what she always said when she was pleased.

"Golly!" said the Match Man. And that was *his* particular phrase.

"Won't you sit down, Moddom?" enquired a voice, and they turned to find a tall man in a black coat coming out of the wood with a table napkin over his arm.

Mary Poppins, thoroughly surprised, sat down with a plop upon one of the little green chairs that stood round the table. The Match Man, staring, collapsed on to another.

"I'm the Waiter, you know!" explained the man in the black coat.

"Oh! But I didn't see you in the picture," said Mary Poppins.

"Ah, I was behind the tree," explained the Waiter.

"Won't you sit down?" said Mary Poppins, politely.

"Waiters never sit down, Moddom," said the man but he seemed pleased at being asked.

"Your whelks, Mister!" he said, pushing a plate of them over to the Match Man. "*And* your Pin!" He dusted the pin on his napkin and handed it to the Match Man.

They began upon the afternoon tea, and the Waiter stood beside them to see they had everything they needed.

"We're having them after all," said Mary Poppins in a loud whisper, as she began on the heap of raspberry-jam cakes.

"Golly!" agreed the Match Man, helping himself to two of the largest.

"Tea?" said the Waiter, filling a large cup for each of them from the urn.

They drank it and had two cups more each, and then, for luck, they finished the pile of raspberry-jam cakes. After that they got up and brushed the crumbs off.

"There is Nothing to Pay," said the Waiter, before they had time to ask for the bill. "It is a Pleasure. You will find the Merry-go-Round just over there!" And he waved his hand to a little gap in the trees, where Mary Poppins and the Match Man could see several wooden horses whirling round on a stand.

"That's funny," said she. "I don't remember seeing that in the picture, either."

"Ah," said the Match Man, who hadn't remembered it himself, "it was in the Background, you see!"

The Merry-go-Round was just slowing down as they approached it.

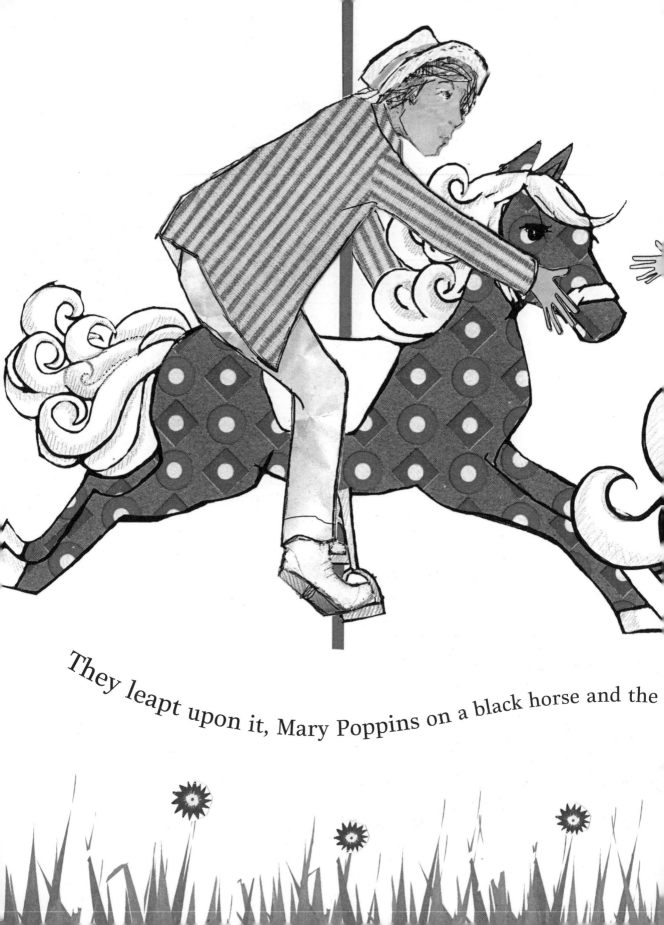

They leapt upon it, Mary Poppins on a black horse and the

Match Man on a grey.

And when the music started again and they began to move, they rode all the way to Yarmouth and back, because that was the place they both wanted most to see.

When they returned it was nearly dark and the Waiter was watching for them.

"I'm very sorry, Moddom and Mister," he said politely, "but we close at Seven. Rules, you know. May I show you the Way Out?"

They nodded as he flourished his table napkin and walked on in front of them through the wood.

"It's a wonderful picture you've drawn this time, Bert," said Mary Poppins, putting her hand through the Match Man's arm and drawing her cloak about her.

"Well, I did my best, Mary," said the Match Man modestly. But you could see he was really very pleased with himself indeed.

Just then the Waiter stopped in front of them, beside a large white doorway that looked as though it were made of thick chalk lines.

"Here you are!"

he said.

"This is the Way Out."

"Goodbye and thank you," said Mary Poppins, shaking his hand.

"Moddom, goodbye!" said the Waiter, bowing so low that his head knocked against his knees.

He nodded to the Match Man, who cocked his head on one side and closed one eye at the Waiter, which was his way of bidding him farewell. Then Mary Poppins stepped through the white doorway and the Match Man followed her.

And as they went, the feather dropped from her hat and the silk cloak from her shoulders and the diamonds from her shoes. The bright clothes of the Match Man faded, and his straw hat turned into his old ragged cap again. Mary Poppins turned and looked at him, and she knew at once what had happened. Standing on the pavement she gazed at him for a long minute, and then her glance explored the wood behind him for the Waiter. But the Waiter was nowhere to be seen. There was nobody in the picture. Nothing moved there. Even the Merry-go-Round had disappeared. Only the still trees and the grass and the unmoving little patch of sea remained.

But Mary Poppins and the Match Man smiled at one another. They knew, you see, what lay behind the trees . . .

When she came back from her Day Out,
  Jane and Michael came running to meet her.

"Where have you been?"
they asked her.

"In Fairyland,"
  said Mary Poppins.

"Did you see Cinderella?" said Jane.

"Huh, Cinderella? Not me,"
said Mary Poppins, contemptuously.
  "Cinderella, indeed!"

"Or Robinson Crusoe?"
asked Michael.

"Robinson Crusoe – pooh!"
said Mary Poppins rudely.

"Then how could you have been there? It couldn't have been *our* Fairyland!"

Mary Poppins gave a superior sniff.

"Don't you know," she said pityingly, "that

everybody's got a *Fairyland* of their own?"

And with another sniff she went upstairs
to take off her white gloves and
put the umbrella away.

THREE

Laughing Gas

"ARE YOU QUITE SURE HE WILL BE AT HOME?" said Jane, as they got off the Bus, she and Michael and Mary Poppins.

"Would my Uncle ask me to bring you to tea if he intended to go out, I'd like to know?" said Mary Poppins, who was evidently very offended by the question. She was wearing her blue coat with the silver buttons and the blue hat to match, and on the days when she wore these it was the easiest thing in the world to offend her.

All three of them were on the way to pay a visit to Mary Poppins's uncle, Mr Wigg, and Jane and Michael had looked forward to the trip for so long that they were more than half afraid that Mr Wigg might not be in, after all.

"Why is he called Mr Wigg – does he wear one?" asked Michael, hurrying along beside Mary Poppins.

"He is called Mr Wigg because Mr Wigg is his name. And he doesn't wear one. He is bald," said Mary Poppins. "And if I have any more questions we will just go Back Home." And she sniffed her usual sniff of displeasure.

Jane and Michael looked at each other and frowned. And the frown meant: "Don't let's ask her anything else or we'll never get there."

Mary Poppins put her hat straight at the Tobacconist's Shop at the corner. It had one of those curious windows where there seem to be three of you instead of one, so that if you look long enough at them you begin to feel you are not yourself but a whole crowd of somebody else. Mary Poppins sighed with pleasure, however, when she saw three of herself, each wearing a blue coat with silver buttons and a blue hat to match. She thought it was such a lovely sight that she wished there had been a dozen of her or even thirty. The more Mary Poppinses the better.

"Come along," she said sternly, as though they had kept *her* waiting. Then they turned the corner and pulled the bell of Number Three, Robertson Road. Jane and Michael could hear it faintly echoing from a long way away and they knew that in one minute, or two at the most, they would be having tea with Mary Poppins's uncle, Mr Wigg, for the first time ever.

"If he's in, of course," Jane said to Michael in a whisper.

At that moment the door flew open and a thin, watery-looking lady appeared.

"Is he in?" said Michael quickly.

"I'll thank you," said Mary Poppins, giving him a terrible glance, "to let *me* do the talking."

"How do you do, Mrs Wigg," said Jane politely.

"Mrs Wigg!" said the thin lady, in a voice even thinner than herself. "How dare you call me Mrs Wigg? No, thank you! I'm plain Miss Persimmon *and* proud of it. Mrs Wigg indeed!" She seemed to be quite upset, and they thought Mr Wigg must be a very odd person if Miss Persimmon was so glad not to be Mrs Wigg.

"Straight up and first door on the landing," said Miss Persimmon, and she went hurrying away down the passage saying:

"Mrs Wigg indeed!"

to herself in a high, thin, outraged voice.

Jane and Michael followed Mary Poppins upstairs. Mary Poppins knocked at the door.

"Come in! Come in! And welcome!" called a loud, cheery voice from inside. Jane's heart was pitter-pattering with excitement.

"He *is* in!" she signalled to Michael with a look.

Mary Poppins opened the door and pushed them in front of her. A large, cheerful room lay before them. At one end of it a fire was burning brightly and in the centre stood an enormous table laid for tea – four cups and saucers, piles of bread and butter, crumpets, coconut cakes and a large plum cake with pink icing.

"Well, this is indeed a Pleasure," a huge voice greeted them, and Jane and Michael looked round for its owner. He was nowhere to be seen. The room appeared to be quite empty. Then they heard Mary Poppins saying crossly:

"Oh, Uncle Albert – not *again*? It's not your birthday, is it?"

And as she spoke she looked up at the ceiling. Jane and Michael looked up too and to their surprise saw a round, fat, bald man who was hanging in the air without holding on to anything. Indeed, he appeared to be *sitting* on the air, for his legs were crossed and he had just put down the newspaper which he had been reading when they came in.

"My dear," said Mr Wigg, smiling down at the children, and looking apologetically at Mary Poppins, "I'm very sorry, but I'm afraid it *is* my birthday."

"Tch, tch, tch!" said Mary Poppins.

"I only remembered last night and there was no time then to send you a postcard asking you to come another day. Very distressing, isn't it?" he said, looking down at Jane and Michael.

"I can see you're rather surprised," said Mr Wigg. And, indeed, their mouths were so wide open with astonishment that Mr Wigg, if he had been a little smaller, might almost have fallen into one of them.

"I'd better explain, I think," Mr Wigg went on calmly. "You see, it's this way. I'm a cheerful sort of man and very disposed to laughter. You wouldn't believe, either of you, the number of things that strike me as being funny. I can laugh at pretty nearly everything, I can."

And with that Mr Wigg began to bob up and down, shaking with laughter at the thought of his own cheerfulness.

"Uncle Albert!"

said Mary Poppins,

and Mr Wigg

stopped laughing

with a jerk.

"Oh, beg pardon, my dear. Where was I? Oh, yes. Well, the funny thing about me is – all right, Mary, I won't laugh if I can help it! – that whenever my birthday falls on a Friday, well, it's all up with me. Absolutely U. P.," said Mr Wigg.

"But why—?" began Jane.

"But how—?" began Michael.

"Well, you see, if I laugh on that particular day I become so filled with Laughing Gas that I simply can't keep on the ground. Even if I smile it happens. The first funny thought, and I'm up like a balloon. And until I can think of something serious I can't get down again." Mr Wigg began to chuckle at that, but he caught sight of Mary Poppins's face and stopped the chuckle, and continued:

"It's awkward, of course, but not unpleasant. Never happens to either of you, I suppose?"

Jane and Michael shook their heads.

"No, I thought not. It seems to be my own special habit. Once, after I'd been to the Circus the night before, I laughed so much that – would you believe it? –

I was up here for a whole twelve hours, and couldn't get down till the last stroke of midnight. Then, of course, I came down with a flop because it was Saturday and not my birthday any more. It's rather odd, isn't it? Not to say funny?

"And now here it is Friday again and my birthday, and you two and Mary P. to visit me. Oh, Lordy, Lordy, don't make me laugh, I beg of you—" But although Jane and Michael had done nothing very amusing, except to stare at him in astonishment, Mr Wigg began to laugh again loudly, and as he laughed he went bouncing and bobbing about in the air, with the newspaper rattling in his hand and his spectacles half on and half off his nose.

He looked so comic, floundering in the air like a great human bubble, clutching at the ceiling sometimes and sometimes at the gas-bracket as he passed it, that Jane and Michael, though they were trying hard to be polite, just couldn't help doing what they did. They laughed.

And they laughed. They shut their mouths tight to prevent the laughter escaping, but that didn't do any good. And presently they were rolling over and over on the floor, squealing and shrieking with laughter.

"Really!" said Mary Poppins. "Really, *such* behaviour!"

"I can't help it, I can't help it!" shrieked Michael, as he rolled into the fender. "It's so terribly funny. Oh, Jane, *isn't* it funny?"

Jane did not reply, for a curious thing was happening to her. As she laughed she felt herself growing lighter and lighter, just as though she were being pumped full of air. It was a curious and delicious feeling and it made her want to laugh all the more. And then suddenly, with a bouncing bounce, she felt herself jumping through the air. Michael, to his astonishment, saw her go soaring up through the room. With a little bump her head touched the ceiling and then she went bouncing along it till she reached Mr Wigg.

"*Well!*" said Mr Wigg, looking very surprised indeed. "Don't tell me it's *your* birthday, too?" Jane shook her head.

"It's not? Then this Laughing Gas must be catching! Hi – whoa there, look out for the mantelpiece!" This was to Michael, who had suddenly risen from the floor and was swooping through the air, roaring with laughter, and just grazing the china ornaments on the mantelpiece as he passed. He landed with a bounce right on Mr Wigg's knee.

"How do you do," said Mr Wigg, heartily shaking Michael by the hand. "I call this really friendly of you – bless my soul, I do! To come up to me since I couldn't come down to you – eh?" And then he and Michael looked at each other and flung back their heads and simply howled with laughter.

"I say," said Mr Wigg to Jane, as he wiped his eyes. "You'll be thinking I have the worst manners in the world. You're standing and you ought to be sitting – a nice young lady like you. I'm afraid I can't offer you a chair up here, but I think you'll find the air quite comfortable to sit on. I do."

Jane tried it and found she could sit down quite comfortably on the air. She took off her hat and laid it down beside her and it hung there in space without any support at all.

"That's right," said Mr Wigg. Then he turned and looked down at Mary Poppins.

"Well, Mary, we're fixed. And now I can enquire about *you*, my dear. I must say, I am very glad to welcome you and my two young friends here today – why, Mary, you're frowning. I'm afraid you don't approve of – er – all this."

He waved his hand at Jane and Michael, and said hurriedly:

"I apologise, Mary, my dear. But you know how it is with me. Still, I must say I never thought my two young friends here would catch it, really I didn't, Mary! I suppose I should have asked them for another day or tried to think of something sad or something—"

"Well, I must say," said Mary Poppins primly, "that I

have never in my life seen such a sight. And at your age, Uncle—"

"Mary Poppins, Mary Poppins, do come up!" interrupted Michael. "Think of something funny and you'll find it's quite easy."

"Ah, now do, Mary!" said Mr Wigg persuasively.

"We're lonely up here without you!" said Jane, and held out her arms towards Mary Poppins. "*Do* think of something funny!"

"Ah, *she* doesn't need to," said Mr Wigg sighing. "She can come up if she wants to, even without laughing – and she knows it." And he looked mysteriously and secretly at Mary Poppins as she stood down there on the hearth rug.

"Well," said Mary Poppins, "it's all very silly and undignified, but, since you're all up there and don't seem able to get down, I suppose I'd better come up, too."

With that, to the surprise of Jane and Michael, she put her hands down at her sides and without a laugh, without even the faintest glimmer of a smile, she shot up through the air and sat down beside Jane.

"How many times, I should like to know," she said snappily, "have I told you to take off your coat when you come into a hot room?" And she unbuttoned Jane's coat and laid it neatly on the air beside the hat.

"That's right, Mary, that's right," said Mr Wigg contentedly, as he leant down and put his spectacles on the mantelpiece. "Now we're all comfortable—"

"There's comfort *and* comfort," sniffed Mary Poppins.

"And we can have tea," Mr Wigg went on, apparently not noticing her remark. And then a startled look came over his face.

"My goodness!" he said. "How dreadful! I've just realised – the table's down there and we're up here. What *are* we going to do? We're here and it's there. It's an awful tragedy – awful! But oh, it's terribly comic!" And he hid his face in his handkerchief and laughed loudly into it. Jane and Michael, though they did not want to miss the crumpets and the cakes, couldn't help laughing too, because Mr Wigg's mirth was so infectious.

Mr Wigg dried his eyes.

"There's only one thing for it," he said. "We must

think of something serious. Something sad, very sad. And then we shall be able to get down. Now – one, two, three! Something *very* sad, mind you!"

They thought and thought, with their chins on their hands.

Michael thought of school, and that one day he would have to go there. But even that seemed funny today and he had to laugh.

Jane thought: "I shall be grown up in another fourteen years!" But that didn't sound sad at all but quite nice and rather funny. She could not help smiling at the thought of herself grown up, with long skirts and a handbag.

"There was my poor old Aunt Emily," thought Mr Wigg out loud. "She was run over by an omnibus. Sad. Very sad. Unbearably sad. Poor Aunt Emily. But they saved her umbrella. That was funny, wasn't it?" And before he knew where he was, he was heaving and trembling and bursting with laughter at the thought of Aunt Emily's umbrella.

"It's no good," he said, blowing his nose. "I give it

up. And my young friends here seem to be no better at sadness than I am. Mary, can't *you* do something? We want our tea."

To this day Jane and Michael cannot be sure of what happened then. All they know for certain is that, as soon as Mr Wigg had appealed to Mary Poppins, the table below began to wriggle on its legs. Presently it was swaying dangerously, and then with a rattle of china and with cakes lurching off their plates on to the cloth, the table came soaring through the room, gave one graceful turn, and landed beside them so that Mr Wigg was at its head.

"Good girl!" said Mr Wigg, smiling proudly upon her. "I knew you'd fix something. Now, will you take

the foot of the table and pour out, Mary? And the guests on either side of me. That's the idea," he said, as Michael ran bobbing through the air and sat down on Mr Wigg's right. Jane was at his left hand. There they were, all together, up in the air and the table between them. Not a single piece of bread-and-butter or a lump of sugar had been left behind.

Mr Wigg smiled contentedly.

"It is usual, I think, to begin with bread-and-butter," he said to Jane and Michael, "but as it's my birthday we will begin the wrong way – which I always think is the right way – with the Cake!"

And he cut a large slice for everybody.

"More tea?" he said to Jane. But before she had time to reply there was a quick, sharp knock at the door.

"Come in!" called Mr Wigg.

The door opened, and there stood Miss Persimmon with a jug of hot water on a tray.

"I thought, Mr Wigg," she began, looking searchingly round the room, "you'd be wanting some more hot— Well, I never! I simply *never*!" she said, as she caught sight of them all seated on the air round the table. "Such goings on I never did see! In all my born days I never saw such. I'm sure, Mr Wigg, I always knew *you* were a bit odd. But I've closed my eyes to it – being as how you paid your rent regular. But such behaviour as this – having tea in the air with your guests – Mr

Wigg, sir, I'm astonished at you! It's that undignified, and for a gentleman of your age – I never did—"

"But perhaps you will, Miss Persimmon!" said Michael.

"Will what?" said Miss Persimmon haughtily.

"Catch the Laughing Gas, as we did," said Michael.

Miss Persimmon flung back her head scornfully.

"I hope, young man," she retorted, "I have more respect for myself than to go bouncing about in the air like a rubber ball on the end of a bat. I'll stay on my own feet, thank you, or my name's not Amy Persimmon, and – oh dear, oh *dear*, my goodness, oh *DEAR* – what is the matter? I can't walk, I'm going, I – oh, help, *HELP!*"

For Miss Persimmon, quite against her will, was off the ground and was stumbling through the air, rolling from side to side like a very thin barrel, balancing the tray in her hand. She was almost weeping with distress as she arrived at the table and put down her jug of hot water.

"Thank you," said Mary Poppins in a calm, very polite voice.

Then Miss Persimmon turned
and went wafting down again,
murmuring as she went:

"So undignified – and me
a well-behaved, steady-going woman.
I must see a doctor—"

When she touched the floor she ran hurriedly out of the room, wringing her hands, and not giving a single glance backwards.

"So undignified!" they heard her moaning as she shut the door behind her.

"Her name can't be Amy Persimmon, because she *didn't* stay on her own feet!" whispered Jane to Michael.

But Mr Wigg was looking at Mary Poppins – a curious look, half amused, half accusing.

"Mary, Mary, you shouldn't – bless my soul, you shouldn't, Mary. The poor old body will never get over it. But, oh, my goodness, didn't she look funny waddling through the air – my Gracious goodness, but didn't she?"

And he and Jane and Michael were off again, rolling about the air, clutching their sides and gasping with laughter at the thought of how funny Miss Persimmon had looked.

"Oh dear!" said Michael. "Don't make me laugh any more. I can't stand it. I shall break!"

"Oh, oh, oh!" cried Jane, as she gasped for breath, with her hand over her heart.

"Oh, my Gracious, Glorious, Galumphing Goodness!" roared Mr Wigg, dabbing his eyes with his coat-tail because he couldn't find his handkerchief.

"IT IS TIME TO GO HOME."

Mary Poppins's voice sounded above the roars of laughter like a trumpet.

And suddenly, with a rush, Jane and Michael and Mr Wigg came down. They landed on the floor with a huge bump, all together. The thought that they would have to go home was the first sad thought of the afternoon, and the moment it was in their minds the Laughing Gas went out of them.

Jane and Michael sighed as they watched Mary Poppins come slowly down the air, carrying Jane's coat and hat.

Mr Wigg sighed, too.

A great, long, heavy sigh.

"Well, isn't that a pity?"

he said soberly.

"It's very sad

that you've

got to go home.

I never

enjoyed

an afternoon

so much –

did you?"

"Never,"

said Michael sadly,

feeling how dull

it was to be

d o w n

on the earth again
with no Laughing Gas
inside him.

"Never, never," said Jane, as she stood on tiptoe and kissed Mr Wigg's withered-apple cheeks.

"Never, never, never, never . . . !"

They sat on either side of Mary Poppins going home in the Bus. They were both very quiet, thinking over the lovely afternoon. Presently Michael said sleepily to Mary Poppins:

"How often does your Uncle get like that?"

"Like what?" said Mary Poppins sharply, as though Michael had deliberately said something to offend her.

"Well – all bouncy and boundy and laughing and going up in the air."

"Up in the air?" Mary Poppins's voice was high and angry. "What do you mean, pray, up in the air?"

Jane tried to explain.

"Michael means – is your Uncle often full of Laughing Gas, and does he often go rolling and bobbing about on the ceiling when—"

"Rolling and bobbing! What an idea! Rolling and bobbing on the ceiling! You'll be telling me next he's a balloon!" Mary Poppins gave an offended sniff.

"But he did!" said Michael. "We saw him."

"What, roll and bob? How dare you! I'll have you know that my Uncle is a sober, honest, hard-working

94

man, and you'll be kind enough to speak of him respectfully. And don't bite your Bus ticket! Roll and bob, indeed – the idea!"

Michael and Jane looked across Mary Poppins at each other. They said nothing, for they had learnt that it was better not to argue with Mary Poppins, no matter how odd anything seemed.

But the look that passed between them said: "Is it true or isn't it? About Mr Wigg. Is Mary Poppins right or are we?"

But there was nobody to give them the right answer.

The Bus roared on, wildly lurching and bounding.

Mary Poppins sat between them, offended and silent, and presently, because they were very tired, they crept closer to her and leant up against her sides and fell asleep, still wondering . . .

Miss Lark's Andrew

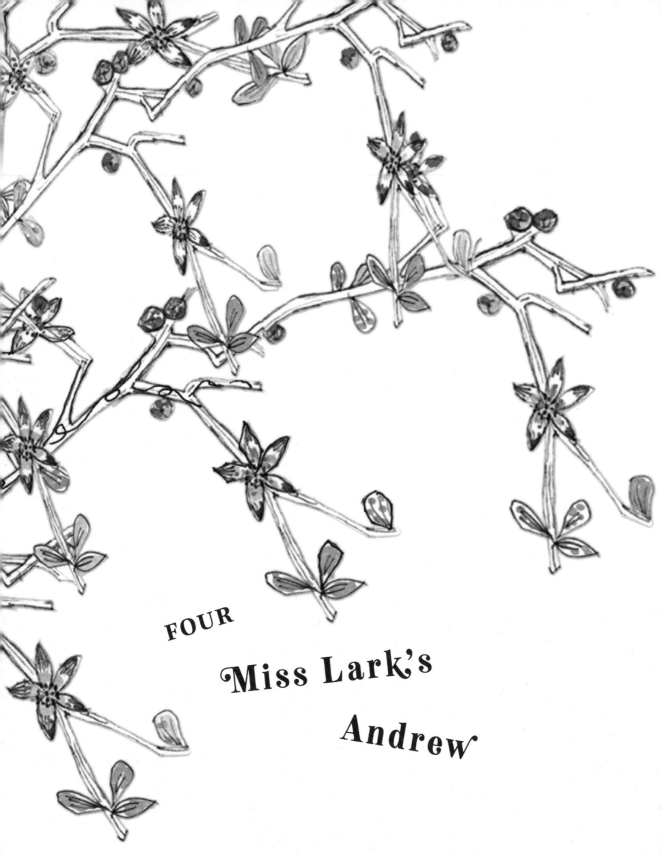

FOUR

Miss Lark's

Andrew

MISS LARK LIVED NEXT DOOR.

But before we go any further I must tell you what Next Door looked like. It was a very grand house, by far the grandest in Cherry Tree Lane. Even Admiral Boom had been known to envy Miss Lark her wonderful house, though his own had ship's funnels instead of chimneys and a flagstaff in the front garden. Over and over again the inhabitants of the Lane heard him say as he rolled past Miss Lark's mansion: "Blast my gizzard! What does *she* want with a house like that?"

And the reason for Admiral Boom's jealousy was that Miss Lark had two gates. One was for Miss Lark's friends and relations, and the other for the Butcher and the Baker and the Milkman.

Once the Baker made a mistake and came in through the gate reserved for the friends and relations, and Miss Lark was so angry that she said she wouldn't have any more bread ever.

But in the end she had to forgive the Baker because he was the only one in the neighbourhood who made those little flat rolls with the curly twists of crust on the top. She never really liked him very much after that, however, and when he came he pulled his hat far down over his eyes so that Miss Lark might think he was somebody else. But she never did.

Jane and Michael always knew when Miss Lark was in the garden or coming along the Lane, because she wore so many brooches and necklaces and earrings that she jingled and jangled just like a brass band. And whenever she met them, she always said the same thing:

"Good morning!" (or "Good afternoon!" if it happened to be after luncheon), "and how are *we* today?"

And Jane and Michael were never quite sure whether Miss Lark was asking how *they* were, or how she and Andrew were.

So they just replied: "Good afternoon!" (or, of course, "Good morning!" if it was before luncheon).

All day long, no matter where the children were, they could hear Miss Lark calling, in a very loud voice, things like:

"Andrew, where are you?"

or

"Andrew, you mustn't go out
without your overcoat!"

or

"Andrew, come to Mother!"

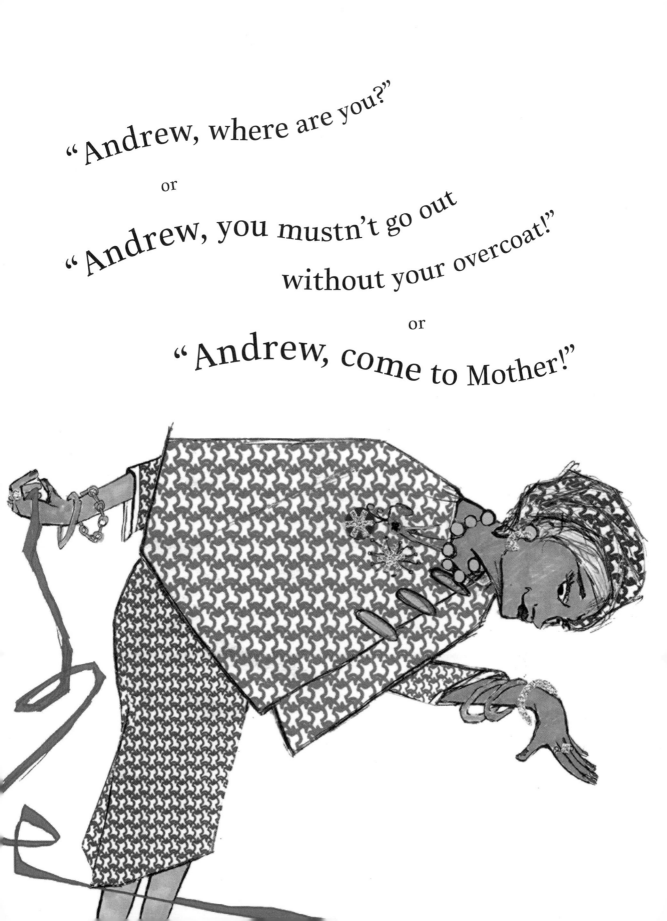

And, if you didn't know, you would think that Andrew must be a little boy. Indeed, Jane thought that Miss Lark thought that Andrew *was* a little boy. But Andrew wasn't. He was a dog – one of those small, silky, fluffy dogs that look like a fur necklet, until they begin to bark. But, of course, when they do that you *know* that they're dogs. No fur necklet ever made a noise like that.

Now, Andrew led such a luxurious life that you might have thought he was the Shah of Persia in disguise. He slept on a silk pillow in Miss Lark's room; he went by car to the Hairdresser's twice a week to be shampooed; he had cream for every meal and sometimes oysters, and he possessed four overcoats with checks and stripes in different colours. Andrew's ordinary days were filled with the kind of things most people have only on birthdays. And when Andrew himself had a birthday he had *two* candles on his cake for every year, instead of only one.

The effect of all this was to make Andrew very much disliked in the neighbourhood. People used to laugh heartily when they saw Andrew sitting up in the back seat of Miss Lark's car on the way to the Hairdresser's, with the fur rug over his knees and his best coat on.

And on the day when Miss Lark bought him two pairs of small leather boots so that he could go out in the Park wet or fine, everybody in the Lane came down to their front gates to watch him go by and to smile secretly behind their hands.

"Pooh!" said Michael, as they were watching Andrew
one day through the fence that separated Number
Seventeen from Next Door. "Pooh, he's a ninkypoop!"

"How do you know?" asked Jane, very interested.

"I know because I heard Daddy call him one this morning!" said Michael, and he laughed at Andrew very rudely.

"He is *not* a nincompoop," said Mary Poppins. "And that is that."

And Mary Poppins was right. Andrew wasn't a nincompoop, as you will very soon see.

You must not think he did not respect Miss Lark. He did. He was even fond of her in a mild sort of way. He couldn't help having a kindly feeling for somebody who had been so good to him ever since he was a puppy, even if she *did* kiss him rather too often. But there was no doubt about it that the life Andrew led bored him to distraction. He would have given half his fortune, if he had one, for a nice piece of raw, red meat, instead of the usual breast of chicken or scrambled eggs with

asparagus.

For in his secret, innermost heart, Andrew longed to be a common dog. He never passed his pedigree (which hung on the wall in Miss Lark's drawing room) without a shudder of shame. And many a time he wished he'd never had a father, nor a grandfather, nor a great-grandfather, if Miss Lark was going to make such a fuss of it.

It was this desire of his to *be* a common dog that made Andrew choose common dogs for his friends. And whenever he got the chance, he would run down to the front gate and sit there watching for them, so that he could exchange a few common remarks. But Miss Lark, when she discovered him, would be sure to call out:

"Andrew, Andrew, come in, my darling!"

And of course Andrew would *have* to come in, or Miss Lark would shame him by coming out and *bringing* him in. And Andrew would blush and hurry up the steps so that his friends should not hear her calling him her Precious, her Joy, her Little Lump of Sugar.

Andrew's most special friend was more than

common, he was a Byword. He was half an Airedale and half a Retriever and the worst half of both. Whenever there was a fight in the road he would be sure to be in the thick of it; he was always getting into trouble with the Postman or the Policeman, and there was nothing he loved better than sniffing about in drains or garbage tins.

He was, in fact, the talk of the whole street, and more than one person had been heard to say thankfully that they were glad he was not *their* dog.

But Andrew loved him and was continually on the watch for him. Sometimes they had only time to exchange a sniff in the Park, but on luckier occasions – though these were very rare – they would have long talks at the gate. From his friend, Andrew heard all the town gossip, and you could see by the rude way in which the other dog laughed as he told it, that it wasn't very complimentary.

Then suddenly, Miss Lark's voice would be heard calling from a window, and the other dog would get up, loll out his tongue at Miss Lark, wink at Andrew and wander off, waving his hindquarters as he went just to show that *he* didn't care.

Andrew, of course, was never allowed outside the gate unless he went with Miss Lark for a walk in the Park, or with one of the maids to have his toes manicured.

Imagine, then, the surprise of Jane and Michael

when they saw Andrew, all alone, careering past them through the Park, with his ears back and his tail up as though he were on the track of a tiger.

Mary Poppins pulled the perambulator up with a jerk, in case Andrew, in his wild flight, should upset it and the Twins. And Jane and Michael screamed at him as he passed.

"Hi, Andrew! Where's your overcoat?" cried Michael, trying to make a high, windy voice like Miss Lark's.

"Andrew, you naughty little boy!" said Jane, and her voice, because she was a girl, was much more like Miss Lark's.

But Andrew just looked at them both very haughtily and barked sharply in the direction of Mary Poppins.

"Yay-yap! Yay-yap! Yay-yap!"

said Andrew several times very quickly.

"Let me see. I think it's the first on your right and second house on the left-hand side," said Mary Poppins.

"Yap?" said Andrew.

"No – no garden. Only a back yard. Gate's usually open."

Andrew barked again.

"I'm not sure," said Mary Poppins. "But I should think so. Generally goes home at tea time."

Andrew flung back his head and set off again at a gallop.

Jane's eyes and Michael's were round as saucers with surprise.

"What was he saying?" they demanded breathlessly, both together.

"Just passing the time of day!" said Mary Poppins, and shut her mouth tightly as though she did not intend any more words to escape from it. John and Barbara gurgled from their perambulator.

"He wasn't!" said Michael.

"He *couldn't* have been!" said Jane.

"Well, you know best, of course.

As usual," said Mary Poppins haughtily.

"He must have been asking you where somebody lived, I'm sure he must—" Michael began.

"Well, if you know, why bother to ask me?" said Mary Poppins, sniffing. "*I'm* no dictionary."

"Oh, Michael," said Jane, "she'll never tell us if you talk like that. Mary Poppins, do say what Andrew was saying to you, *please*."

"Ask *him*. He knows – Mr Know-All!" said Mary Poppins, nodding her head scornfully at Michael.

"Oh no, I don't. I promise I don't, Mary Poppins. Do tell."

"Half past three. Tea time," said Mary Poppins, and she wheeled the perambulator round and shut her mouth tight again as though it were a trap door. She did not say another word all the way home.

Jane dropped behind with Michael.

"It's your fault!" she said. "Now we'll never know."

"I don't care!" said Michael, and he began to push his scooter very quickly. "I don't want to know."

But he did want to know very badly indeed. And as it turned out, he and Jane and everybody else knew all about it before tea time.

Just as they were about to cross the road to their own house, they heard loud cries coming from Next Door, and there they saw a curious sight. Miss Lark's two maids were rushing wildly about the garden, looking under bushes and up into the trees as people do who have lost their most valuable possession. And there was Robertson Ay, from Number Seventeen, busily wasting his time by poking at the gravel on Miss Lark's path with a broom as though he expected to find the missing treasure under a pebble. Miss Lark herself was running about in her garden, waving her arms and calling: "Andrew, Andrew! Oh, he's lost. My darling boy is lost! We must send for the Police. I must see the Prime Minister. Andrew is lost! Oh dear! Oh dear!"

"Oh, poor Miss Lark!" said Jane, hurrying across the road. She could not help feeling sorry because Miss Lark looked so upset.

But it was Michael who really comforted Miss Lark. Just as he was going in at the gate of Number Seventeen, he looked down the Lane and there he saw—

"Why, there's Andrew, Miss Lark. See, down there – just turning Admiral Boom's corner!"

"Where, where? Show me!" said Miss Lark breathlessly, and she peered in the direction in which Michael was pointing.

And there, sure enough, *was* Andrew, walking as slowly and as casually as though nothing in the world was the matter; and beside him waltzed a huge dog that seemed to be half an Airedale and half a Retriever, and the worst half of both.

"Oh, what a relief!" said Miss Lark, sighing loudly. "What a load off my mind!"

Mary Poppins and the children waited in the Lane outside Miss Lark's gate. Miss Lark herself and her two maids leant over the fence, Robertson Ay, resting from his labours, propped himself up with his broom-handle, and all of them watched in silence the return of Andrew.

He and his friend marched sedately up to the group, whisking their tails jauntily and keeping their ears well cocked, and you could tell by the look in Andrew's eye that, whatever he meant, he meant business.

"That dreadful dog!" said Miss Lark, looking at Andrew's companion. "Shoo! Shoo! Go home!" she cried.

But the dog just sat down on the pavement and scratched his right ear with his left leg and yawned.

"Go away! Go home! Shoo, I say!"

said Miss Lark,

waving her arms angrily at the dog.

"And you, Andrew," she went on, "come indoors this minute! Going out like that – all alone and without your overcoat. I am very displeased with you!"

Andrew barked lazily, but did not move.

"What do you mean, Andrew? Come in at once!" said Miss Lark.

Andrew barked again.

"He says," put in Mary Poppins, "that he's not coming in."

Miss Lark turned and regarded her haughtily. "How do *you* know what my dog says, may I ask? Of course he will come in."

Andrew, however, merely shook his head and gave one or two low growls.

"He won't," said Mary Poppins. "Not unless his friend comes, too."

"Stuff and nonsense," said Miss Lark crossly. "That *can't* be what he says. As if I could have a great hulking mongrel like that inside my gate."

Andrew yapped three or four times.

"He says he means it," said Mary Poppins. "And what's more, he'll go and live with his friend unless his friend is allowed to come and live with him."

"Oh, Andrew, you can't – you can't, really – after all I've done for you and everything!" Miss Lark was nearly weeping.

Andrew barked and turned away. The other dog got up.

"Oh, he *does* mean it!" cried Miss Lark. "I see he does. He is going away." She sobbed a moment into her handkerchief, then she blew her nose and said:

"Very well, then, Andrew. I give in. This – this common dog can stay. On condition, of course, that he sleeps in the coal-cellar."

"He insists, ma'am, that that won't do. His friend must have a silk cushion just like his and sleep in your room too. Otherwise he will go and sleep in the coal-cellar with his friend," said Mary Poppins.

"Andrew, how could you?" moaned Miss Lark. "I shall never consent to such a thing."

Andrew looked as though he were preparing to depart. So did the other dog.

"Oh, he's leaving me!" shrieked Miss Lark. "Very well, then, Andrew. It will be as you wish. He *shall* sleep in my room. But I shall never be the same again, never, never. Such a common dog!"

She wiped her streaming eyes and went on:

"I should never have thought it of you, Andrew. But I'll say no more, no matter what I think. And this – er – creature – I shall have to call Waif or Stray or—"

At that the other dog looked at Miss Lark very indignantly, and Andrew barked loudly.

"They say you must call him Willoughby and nothing else," said Mary Poppins. "Willoughby being his name."

"Willoughby! What a name! Worse and worse!" said Miss Lark despairingly. "What is he saying now?" For Andrew was barking again.

"He says that if he comes back you are never to make him wear overcoats or go to the Hairdresser's again – that's his last word," said Mary Poppins.

There was a pause.

"Very well," said Miss Lark at last. "But I warn you, Andrew, if you catch your death of cold – don't blame me!"

And with that she turned and walked haughtily up the steps, sniffing away the last of her tears.

Andrew cocked his head towards Willoughby as if to say: "Come on!" and the two of them waltzed side by side slowly up the garden path, waving their tails like banners, and followed Miss Lark into the house.

"He isn't a ninkypoop after all, you see," said Jane, as they went upstairs to the Nursery and Tea.

"No," agreed Michael. "But how do you think Mary Poppins knew?"

"I don't know," said Jane. "And she'll never, never tell us. I am sure of that . . ."

The Bird

Woman

FIVE The Bird Woman

"PERHAPS SHE WON'T BE THERE," SAID MICHAEL.

"Yes, she will," said Jane. "She's always there for ever and ever."

They were walking up Ludgate Hill on the way to pay a visit to Mr Banks in the City. For he had said that morning to Mrs Banks:

"My dear, if it doesn't rain I think Jane and Michael might call for me at the Office today – that is, if you are agreeable. I have a feeling I should like to be taken to Tea and Shortbread Fingers and it's not often I have a Treat."

And Mrs Banks had said she would think about it.

124

But all day long, though Jane and Michael had watched her anxiously, she had not seemed to be thinking about it at all. From the things she said, she was thinking about the Laundry Bill and Michael's new overcoat and where was Aunt Flossie's address, and why did that wretched Mrs Jackson ask her to tea on the second Thursday of the month when she knew that was the very day Mrs Banks had to go to the Dentist's?

Suddenly, when they felt quite sure she would never think about Mr Banks's treat, she said:

"Now, children, don't stand staring at me like that. Get your things on. You are going to the City to have tea with your Father. Had you forgotten?"

As if they could have forgotten! For it was not as though it were only the Tea that mattered. There was also the Bird Woman, and she herself was the best of all Treats.

That is why they were walking up Ludgate Hill and feeling very excited.

Mary Poppins walked between them, wearing her new hat and looking very distinguished. Every now and then she would look into the shop window just to make sure the hat was still there and that the pink roses on it had not turned into common flowers like marigolds.

Every time she stopped to make sure, Jane and Michael would sigh, but they did not dare say anything for fear she would spend even longer looking at herself in the windows, and turning this way and that to see which attitude was the most becoming.

But at last they came to St Paul's Cathedral, which was built a long time ago by a man with a bird's name. Wren it was, but he was no relation to Jenny. That is why so many birds live near Sir Christopher Wren's

Cathedral, which also belongs to St Paul, and that is why the Bird Woman lives there, too.

"There she is!" cried Michael suddenly, and he danced on his toes with excitement.

"Don't point," said Mary Poppins, giving a last glance at the pink roses in the window of a carpet shop.

"She's saying it! She's saying it!" cried Jane, holding tight to herself for fear she would break in two with delight.

And she *was* saying it. The Bird Woman was there and she was saying it.

"Feed the Birds, Tuppence a Bag!
Feed the Birds, Tuppence a Bag!
Feed the Birds, Feed the Birds,
Tuppence a Bag, Tuppence a Bag!"

Over and over again, the same thing, in a high chanting voice that made the words seem like a song.

And as she said it she held out little bags of breadcrumbs to the passers-by.

All round her flew the birds, circling and leaping and swooping and rising. Mary Poppins always called them "sparrers" because, she said conceitedly, all birds were alike to her. But Jane and Michael knew that they were not sparrows, but doves and pigeons. There were fussy and chatty grey doves like Grandmothers; and brown, rough-voiced pigeons like Uncles; and greeny, cackling, no-I've-no-money-today pigeons like Fathers. And the silly, anxious, soft blue doves were like Mothers. That's what Jane and Michael thought, anyway.

They flew round and round the head of the Bird Woman as the children approached, and then, as though to tease her, they suddenly rushed away through the air and sat on the top of St Paul's, laughing and turning their heads away and pretending they didn't know her.

It was Michael's turn to buy a bag. Jane had bought one last time. He walked up to the Bird Woman and held out four halfpennies.

"*Feed* the Birds, Tuppence a Bag!" said the Bird Woman, as she put a bag of crumbs into his hand and tucked the money away into the folds of her huge black skirt.

"Why don't you have penny bags?" said Michael. "Then I could buy two."

"Feed the Birds, *Tuppence* a Bag!" said the Bird Woman, and Michael knew it was no good asking her any more questions. He and Jane had often tried, but all she could say, and all she had ever been able to say, was, "Feed the Birds, Tuppence a Bag!" Just as a cuckoo can only say "Cuckoo," no matter what questions you ask him.

Jane and Michael and Mary Poppins spread the crumbs in a circle on the ground, and presently, one by one at first, and then in twos and threes, the birds came down from St Paul's.

"Dainty David," said Mary Poppins with a sniff, as one bird picked up a crumb and dropped it again from its beak.

But the other birds swarmed upon the food, pushing and scrambling and shouting. At last there wasn't a crumb left, for it is not really polite for a pigeon or a dove to leave anything on the plate. When they were quite certain that the meal was finished the birds rose with one grand, fluttering movement and flew round the Bird Woman's head, copying in their own language the words she said. One of them sat on her hat and pretended he was a decoration for the crown. And another of them mistook Mary Poppins's new hat for a rose garden and pecked off a flower.

"You sparrer!" cried Mary Poppins, and shook her umbrella at him.

The pigeon, very offended, flew back to the Bird Woman, and to pay out Mary Poppins, stuck the rose in the ribbon of the Bird Woman's hat.

"You ought to be in a pie – that's where *you* ought to be," said Mary Poppins to him very angrily. Then she called to Jane and Michael.

"Time to go," she said, and flung a parting glance of fury at the pigeon. But he only laughed and flicked his tail and turned his back on her.

"Goodbye," said Michael to the Bird Woman.

"Feed the Birds," she replied, smiling.

"Goodbye," said Jane.

"Tuppence a Bag!" said the Bird Woman and waved her hand.

They left her then, walking one on either side of Mary Poppins.

"What happens when *everybody* goes away – like us?" said Michael to Jane.

He knew quite well what happened, but it was the proper thing to ask Jane because the story was really hers.

So Jane told him and he added the bits she had forgotten.

"At night when everybody goes to bed—" began Jane.

"And the stars come out," added Michael.

"Yes, and even if they don't – all the birds come down from the top of St Paul's and run very carefully all over the ground just to see there are no crumbs left, and to tidy it up for the morning. And when they have done that—"

"You've forgotten the baths."

"Oh, yes – they bath themselves and comb their wings with their claws. And when they have done that they fly three times round the head of the Bird Woman and then they settle."

"Do they sit on her shoulders?"

"Yes, and on her hat."

"And on her basket with the bags in it?"

"Yes, and some on her knee. Then she smooths down the head-feathers of each one in turn and tells it to be a good bird—"

"In the bird language?"

"Yes. And when they are all sleepy and don't want to stay awake any longer, she spreads out her skirts, as a mother hen spreads out her wings, and the birds go creep, creep, creeping underneath. And as soon as the last one is under she settles down over them, making little brooding, nesting noises, and they sleep there till morning."

Michael sighed happily. He loved the story and was never tired of hearing it.

"And it's all quite true, isn't it?" he said, just as he always did.

"No," said Mary Poppins, who always said "No".

"Yes," said Jane, who always knew everything . . .

John and Barbara's Story

SIX

John

and

Barbara's

Story

JANE AND MICHAEL HAD GONE OFF TO A PARTY, wearing their best clothes and looking, as Ellen the housemaid said when she saw them, "just like a shop window".

All the afternoon the house was very quiet and still, as though it were thinking its own thoughts, or dreaming perhaps.

Down in the kitchen Mrs Brill was reading the paper with her spectacles perched on her nose. Robertson Ay was sitting in the garden busily doing nothing. Mrs Banks was on the drawing-room sofa with her feet up. And the house stood very quietly around them all, dreaming its own dreams, or thinking perhaps.

Upstairs in the Nursery Mary Poppins was airing the clothes by the fire, and the sunlight poured in at the window, flickering on the white walls, dancing over the cots where the babies were lying.

"I say, move over! You're right in my eyes," said John in a loud voice.

"Sorry!" said the sunlight. "But I can't help it. I've got to get across this room somehow. Orders is orders.

I must move from East to West in a day and my way lies through this Nursery. Sorry! Shut your eyes and you won't notice me."

The gold shaft of sunlight lengthened across the room. It was obviously moving as quickly as it could in order to oblige John.

"How soft, how sweet you are! I love you," said Barbara, holding out her hands to its shining warmth.

"Good girl," said the sunlight approvingly, and moved up over her cheeks and into her hair with a light, caressing movement. "Do you like the feel of me?" it said, as though it loved being praised.

"Dee-licious!" said Barbara, with a happy sigh.

"Chatter, chatter, chatter! I never heard such a place for chatter. There's always somebody talking in this room," said a shrill voice at the window.

John and Barbara looked up.

It was the Starling who lived on the top of the chimney.

"I like that," said Mary Poppins, turning round quickly. "What about yourself? All day long – yes, and half the night, too, on the roofs and telegraph poles.

Roaring and screaming and shouting – you'd talk the leg off a chair, you would. Worse than any sparrer, and that's the truth."

The Starling cocked his head on one side and looked down at her from his perch on the window frame.

"Well," he said, "I have my business to attend to. Consultations, discussions, arguments, bargaining. And that, of course, necessitates a certain amount of – er – quiet conversation—"

"Quiet!" exclaimed John, laughing heartily.

"And I wasn't talking to you, young man," said the Starling, hopping down on to the windowsill. "And *you* needn't talk – anyway. I heard you for several hours on end last Saturday week. Goodness, I thought you'd never stop – you kept me awake all night."

"That wasn't talking," said John. "I was—" He paused. "I mean, I had a pain."

"Humph!" said the Starling, and hopped on to the railing of Barbara's cot. He sidled along it until he came to the head of the cot. Then he said in a soft, wheedling voice:

"Well, Barbara B., anything for the old fellow today, eh?"

Barbara pulled herself into a sitting position by holding on to one of the bars of her cot.

"There's the other half of my arrowroot biscuit," she said, and held it out in her round, fat fist.

The Starling swooped down, plucked it out of her hand and flew back to the windowsill. He began nibbling it greedily.

"Thank you!" said Mary Poppins, meaningly, but the Starling was too busy eating to notice the rebuke.

"I said 'Thank you!'" said Mary Poppins a little louder. The Starling looked up.

"Eh – what? Oh, get along, girl, get along. I've no time for such frills and furbelows."

And he gobbled up all but the last crumbs of his biscuit.

The room was very quiet.

John, drowsing in the sunlight, put the toes of his right foot into his mouth and ran them along the place where his teeth were just beginning to come through.

"Why do you bother to do that?" said Barbara, in her soft, amused voice that seemed always to be full of laughter. "There's nobody to see you."

"I know," said John, playing a tune on his toes. "But I like to keep in practice. It *does* so amuse the Grown-ups. Did you notice that Aunt Flossie nearly went mad with delight when I did it yesterday? 'The Darling, the Clever, the Marvel, the Creature!' – didn't you hear her say all that?" And John threw his foot from him and roared with laughter as he thought of Aunt Flossie.

"She liked my trick, too," said Barbara complacently. "I took off both my socks and she said I was so sweet she would like to eat me. Isn't it funny – when *I* say I'd like to eat something I really mean it. Biscuits and Rusks and the knobs of beds and so on. But Grown-ups never mean what they say, it seems to me. She couldn't have *really* wanted to eat me, could she?"

"No. It's only the idiotic way they have of talking," said John. "I don't believe I'll ever understand Grown-ups. They all seem so stupid. And even Jane and Michael are stupid sometimes."

"Um," agreed Barbara, thoughtfully pulling off her socks.

"For instance," John went on, "they don't understand a single thing we say. But, worse than that, they don't understand what *other* things say. Why, only last Monday I heard Jane remark that she wished she knew what language the Wind spoke."

"I know," said Barbara. "It's astonishing. And Michael always insists – haven't you heard him? – that the Starling says 'Wee-Twe – ee – ee!' He seems not to know that the Starling says nothing of the kind, but speaks exactly the same language as we do. Of course, one doesn't expect Mother and Father to know about it – they don't know *anything*, though they *are* such darlings – but you'd think Jane and Michael would—"

"They did once," said Mary Poppins, folding up one of Jane's nightgowns.

"What?" said John and Barbara together in very surprised voices. "Really? You mean they understood the Starling and the Wind and—"

"And what the trees say and the language of the sunlight and the stars – of course they did! *Once,*" said Mary Poppins.

"But – how is it that they've forgotten it all?" said John, wrinkling up his forehead and trying to understand.

"Aha!" said the Starling knowingly, looking up from the remains of his biscuit. "Wouldn't you like to know?"

"Because they've grown older," explained Mary Poppins. "Barbara, put on your socks at once, please."

"That's a silly reason," said John, looking sternly at her.

"It's the true one, then," Mary Poppins said, tying Barbara's socks firmly round her ankles.

"Well, it's Jane and Michael who are silly," John continued. "I know *I* shan't forget when *I* get older."

"Nor I," said Barbara, contentedly sucking her finger.

"Yes, you will," said Mary Poppins firmly.

The Twins sat up and looked at her.

"Huh!" said the Starling contemptuously. "Look at 'em! They think they're the World's Wonders. Little miracles – I *don't* think! Of course you'll forget – same as Jane and Michael."

"We *won't*," said the Twins, looking at the Starling as if they would like to murder him.

The Starling jeered.

"I say you will," he insisted. "It isn't your fault, of course," he added more kindly. "You'll forget because you just can't help it. There never was a human being that remembered after the age of one – at the very latest – except, of course, Her." And he jerked his head over his shoulder at Mary Poppins.

"But why can she remember and not us?" said John.

"A-a-a-h! She's different. She's the Great Exception. Can't go by *her*," said the Starling, grinning at them both.

John and Barbara were silent.

The Starling went on explaining.

"She's something special, you see.

Not in the matter of looks, of course.

One of my own day-old chicks

is handsomer than

Mary P. ever was—"

"Here, you impertinence!"

said Mary Poppins

crossly,

making a dart at him

and flicking

her apron

in

his

direction.

But the Starling leapt aside
and flew up to the window frame,
whistling wickedly, well out of reach.

"Thought you had me that time, didn't you?"

he jeered and shook his wing-feathers at her.

Mary Poppins snorted.

The sunlight moved on through the room, drawing its long gold shaft after it. Outside a light wind had sprung up and was whispering gently to the cherry trees in the Lane.

"Listen, listen, the wind's talking," said John, tilting his head on one side. "Do you really mean we won't be able to hear *that* when we're older, Mary Poppins?"

"You'll hear all right," said Mary Poppins, "but you won't understand." At that Barbara began to weep gently. There were tears in John's eyes, too. "Well, it can't be helped. It's how things happen," said Mary Poppins sensibly.

"Look at them, just look at them!" jeered the Starling. "Crying fit to kill themselves! Why, a starling in the egg's got more sense. Look at them!"

For John and Barbara were now crying piteously in their cots – long-drawn sobs of deep unhappiness.

Suddenly the door opened and in came Mrs Banks.

"I thought I heard the babies," she said. Then she ran to the Twins. "What is it, my darlings?

Oh, my Treasures, my Sweets, my Love-birds, what is it? Why are they crying so, Mary Poppins?

They've been so quiet all afternoon – not a sound out of them. What can be the matter?"

"Yes, ma'am. No, ma'am. I expect they're getting their teeth, ma'am," said Mary Poppins, deliberately not looking in the direction of the Starling.

"Oh, of course – that must be it," said Mrs Banks brightly.

"I don't want teeth if they make me forget all the things I like best," wailed John, tossing about in his cot.

"Neither do I," wept Barbara, burying her face in her pillow.

"My poor ones, my pets – it will be all right when the naughty old teeth come through," said Mrs Banks soothingly, going from one cot to the other.

"You don't understand!" roared John furiously. "I don't *want* teeth."

"It won't be all right, it will be all *wrong*!" wailed Barbara to her pillow.

"Yes – yes. There – there. Mother knows – Mother understands. It will be all right when the teeth come through," crooned Mrs Banks tenderly.

A faint noise came from the window. It was the Starling hurriedly swallowing a laugh. Mary Poppins gave him one look. That sobered him, and he continued to regard the scene without the hint of a smile.

Mrs Banks was patting her children gently, first one and then the other, and murmuring words that were meant to be reassuring. Suddenly John stopped crying. He had very good manners, and he was fond of his Mother and remembered what was due to her. It was not *her* fault, poor woman, that she always said the wrong thing. It was just, he reflected, that she did not understand. So, to show that he forgave her, he turned over on his back, and very dolefully, sniffing back his tears, he picked up his right foot in both hands and ran his toes along his open mouth.

"Clever One, oh, Clever One," said his Mother admiringly. He did it again and she was very pleased.

Then Barbara, not to be outdone in courtesy, came out of her pillow and with her tears still wet on her face, sat up and plucked off both her socks.

"Wonderful girl," said Mrs Banks proudly, and kissed her.

"There, you see, Mary Poppins! They're quite good again. I can always comfort them. Quite good, quite good," said Mrs Banks, as though she were singing a lullaby. "And the teeth will soon be through."

"Yes, ma'am," said Mary Poppins quietly; and smiling to the Twins, Mrs Banks went out and closed the door.

The moment she had disappeared the Starling burst into a peal of rude laughter.

"Excuse me smiling!" he cried. "But really – I can't help it. What a scene! *What* a scene!"

John took no notice of him. He pushed his face through the bars of his cot and called softly and fiercely to Barbara:

"I *won't* be like the others. I tell you I won't. They," he jerked his head towards the Starling and Mary Poppins, "can say what they like. I'll never forget, *never!*"

Mary Poppins smiled, a secret, I-know-better-than-you

sort of smile, all to herself.

"Nor I," answered Barbara. "Ever."

"Bless my tail-feathers – listen to them!" shrieked the Starling, as he put his wings on his hips and roared with mirth. "As if they could help forgetting! Why, in a month or two – three at the *most* – they won't even know what my name is – silly cuckoos! Silly, half-grown featherless cuckoos! Ha! Ha! Ha!" And with another loud peal of laughter he spread his speckled wings and flew out of the window.

It was not very long afterwards that the teeth, after much trouble, came through as all teeth must, and the Twins had their first birthday.

The day after the birthday party the Starling, who had been away on holiday at Bournemouth, came back to Number Seventeen, Cherry Tree Lane.

"Hullo, hullo, hullo!
Here we are again!"

he screamed joyfully,

landing with a little wobble upon the windowsill.

"Well, how's the girl?" he enquired cheekily of Mary Poppins, cocking his little head on one side and regarding her with bright, amused, twinkling eyes.

"None the better for *your* asking," said Mary Poppins, tossing her head.

The Starling laughed.

"Same old Mary P.," he said. "No change out of *you*! How are the other ones – the cuckoos?" he asked, and looked across at Barbara's cot.

"Well, Barbarina," he began in his soft, wheedling voice, "anything for the old fellow today?"

"Be-lah-belah-belah-belah!" said Barbara, crooning gently as she continued to eat her arrowroot biscuit.

The Starling, with a start of surprise, hopped a little nearer.

"I said," he repeated more distinctly, "is there anything for the old fellow today, Barbie dear?"

"Ba-loo – ba-loo – ba-loo!"

murmured Barbara, gazing up at the ceiling as she swallowed the last sweet crumb.

The Starling stared at her.

"Ha!" he said suddenly, and turned and looked enquiringly at Mary Poppins. Her quiet glance met his in a long look.

Then with a darting movement the Starling flew over to John's cot and alighted on the rail. John had a large woolly lamb hugged close in his arms.

"What's my name? What's my name? What's my name?" cried the Starling in a shrill, anxious voice.

"Er-umph!" said John, opening his mouth and putting the leg of the woolly lamb into it.

With a little shake of the head the Starling turned away.

"So – it's happened," he said quietly to Mary Poppins. She nodded.

The Starling gazed dejectedly for a moment at the Twins. Then he shrugged his speckled shoulders.

"Oh, well – I knew it would. Always told 'em so. But they wouldn't believe it." He remained silent for a little while, staring into the cots. Then he shook himself vigorously.

"Well, well. I must be off. Back to my chimney. It will need a spring-cleaning, I'll be bound." He flew on to the windowsill and paused, looking back over his shoulder.

"It'll seem funny without them, though. Always liked talking to them – so I did. I shall miss them."

He brushed his wing quickly across his eyes.

"Crying?" jeered Mary Poppins. The Starling drew himself up.

"Crying? Certainly not. I have – er – a slight cold, caught on my return journey – that's all. Yes, a slight cold. Nothing serious."

He darted up to the windowpane,

brushed down his breast-feathers

with his beak

and then,

"Cheerio!"

he said perkily,

and spread his wings and was gone . . .

n d.

SEVEN

West Wind

IT WAS THE FIRST DAY OF SPRING.

Jane and Michael knew this at once, because they heard Mr Banks singing in his bath, and there was only one day in the year when he did that.

They always remembered that particular morning. For one thing, it was the first time they were allowed to come downstairs for breakfast, and for another

Mr Banks lost his black bag. So that the day began with two extraordinary happenings.

"Where is my *BAG?*"

shouted Mr Banks, turning round and round in the hall like a dog chasing its tail.

And everybody else began running round and round, too – Ellen and Mrs Brill and the children. Even Robertson Ay made a special effort and turned round twice. At last Mr Banks discovered the bag himself in his study, and he rushed into the hall with it, holding it aloft.

"Now," he said, as though he were delivering a sermon, "my bag is always kept in one place. Here. On the umbrella stand. Who put it in the study?" he roared.

"You did, my dear, when you took the Income Tax papers out of it last night," said Mrs Banks.

Mr Banks gave her such a hurt look that she wished she had been less tactless and had said she had put it there herself.

"Humph – urrumph!" he said, blowing his nose very hard and taking his overcoat from its peg. He walked with it to the front door.

"Hullo," he said more cheerfully, "the Parrot tulips are in bud!" He went into the garden and sniffed the air.

"H'm, wind's in the West, I think."

He looked down towards Admiral Boom's house where the telescope weathercock swung. "I thought so," he said. "Westerly weather. Bright and balmy. I won't take an overcoat."

And with that he picked up his bag and his bowler hat and hurried away to the City.

"Did you hear what he said?" Michael grabbed Jane's arm.

She nodded. "The wind's in the West," she said slowly.

Neither of them said any more, but there was a thought in each of their minds that they wished was not there.

They forgot it soon, however, for everything seemed to be as it always was, and the Spring sunlight lit up the house so beautifully that nobody remembered it needed a coat of paint and new wallpapers. On the contrary, they all found themselves thinking that it was the best house in Cherry Tree Lane.

But trouble began after luncheon.

Jane had gone down to dig in the garden with Robertson Ay. She had just sown a row of radish seed when she heard a great commotion in the Nursery and the sound of hurrying footsteps on the stairs. Presently Michael appeared, very red in the face and panting loudly.

"Look, Jane, look!" he cried, and held out his hand. Within it lay Mary Poppins's compass, with the disc frantically swinging round the arrow as it trembled in Michael's shaking hand.

"The compass?" said Jane, and looked at him questioningly.

Michael suddenly burst into tears.

"She gave it to me," he wept. "She said I could have it all for myself now. Oh, oh, there must be something wrong! What is going to happen? She has never given me anything before."

"Perhaps she was only being nice," said Jane to soothe him, but in her heart she felt as disturbed as Michael was. She knew very well that Mary Poppins never wasted time in being nice.

And yet, strange to say, during that afternoon Mary Poppins never said a cross word. Indeed, she hardly said a word at all. She seemed to be thinking very deeply, and when they asked questions she answered them in a far-away voice. At last Michael could bear it no longer.

"Oh, do be cross, Mary Poppins! Do be cross again! It is not like you. Oh, I feel so anxious." And indeed, his heart felt heavy with the thought that something, he did not quite know what, was about to happen at Number Seventeen, Cherry Tree Lane.

"Trouble trouble and it will trouble you!" retorted Mary Poppins crossly, in her usual voice.

And immediately he felt a little better.

"Perhaps it's only a feeling," he said to Jane. "Perhaps everything is all right and I'm just imagining – don't you think so, Jane?"

"Probably," said Jane slowly. But she was thinking hard and her heart felt tight in her body.

The wind grew wilder towards evening, and blew in little gusts about the house. It went pulling and whistling down the chimneys, slipping through the cracks under the windows, turning the Nursery carpet up at the corners.

Mary Poppins gave them their supper and cleared away the things, stacking them neatly and methodically. Then she tidied up the Nursery and put the kettle on the hob.

"There!" she said, glancing round the room to see that everything was all right. She was silent for a minute. Then she put one hand lightly on Michael's head and the other on Jane's shoulder.

"Now," she said, "I am just going to take the shoes down for Robertson Ay to clean. Behave yourselves, please, till I come back." She went out and shut the door quietly behind her.

Suddenly, as she went, they both felt they must run after her, but something seemed to stop them. They remained quiet, with their elbows on the table, waiting for her to come back. Each was trying to reassure the other without saying anything.

"How silly we are," said Jane presently. "Everything's all right." But she knew she said it more to comfort Michael than because she thought it was true.

The Nursery clock ticked loudly from the mantelpiece. The fire flickered and crackled and slowly died down. They still sat there at the table, waiting.

At last Michael said uneasily: "She's been gone a very long time, hasn't she?"

The wind whistled and cried about the house as if in reply. The clock went on ticking its solemn double note.

Suddenly the silence was broken by the sound of the front door shutting with a loud bang.

"Michael!" said Jane, starting up.

"Jane!" said Michael, with a white, anxious look on his face.

They listened. Then they ran quickly to the window and looked out.

Down below, just outside the front door, stood Mary Poppins, dressed in her coat and hat, with her carpet bag in one hand and her umbrella in the other. The wind was blowing wildly about her, tugging at her skirt, tilting her hat rakishly to one side. But it seemed to Jane and Michael that she did not mind, for she smiled as though she and the wind understood each other.

She paused for a moment on the step and glanced back towards the front door. Then with a quick movement she opened the umbrella, though it was not raining, and thrust it over her head.

The wind, with a wild cry, slipped under the umbrella, pressing it upwards as though trying to force it out of Mary Poppins's hand. But she held on tightly, and that, apparently, was what the wind wanted her to do, for presently it lifted the umbrella higher into the air and Mary Poppins from the ground. It carried her lightly so that her toes just grazed along the garden path. Then it lifted her over the front gate and swept her upwards towards the branches of the cherry trees in the Lane.

"She's going, Jane, she's going!" cried Michael, weeping.

"Quick!" cried Jane. "Let us get the Twins. They must see the last of her." She had no doubt now, nor had Michael, that Mary Poppins had gone for good because the wind had changed.

They each seized a Twin and rushed back to the window.

Mary Poppins was in the upper air now, floating away over the cherry trees and the roofs of the houses, holding tightly to the umbrella with one hand and to the carpet bag with the other.

The Twins began to cry quietly.

With their free hands Jane and Michael opened the window and made one last effort to stay Mary Poppins's flight.

"Mary Poppins!" they cried.

"Mary Poppins, come back!"

But she either did not hear or deliberately took no notice. For she went sailing on and on, up into the cloudy, whistling air, till at last she was wafted away over the hill and the children could see nothing but the trees bending and moaning under the wild west wind . . .

"She did what she said she would, anyway. She stayed till the wind changed," said Jane, sighing and turning sadly from the window. She took John to his cot and put him into it. Michael said nothing, but as he brought Barbara back and tucked her into bed he was sniffing uncomfortably.

"I wonder," said Jane, "if we'll ever see her again?"

Suddenly they heard voices on the stairs.

"Children, children!" Mrs Banks was calling as she opened the door. "Children – I am very cross. Mary Poppins has left us—"

"Yes," said Jane and Michael.

"You knew, then?" said Mrs Banks, rather surprised. "Did she tell you she was going?"

They shook their heads, and Mrs Banks went on:

"It's outrageous. One minute here and gone the next. Not even an apology. Simply said, 'I'm going!' and off she went. Anything more preposterous, more thoughtless, more discourteous— What is it, Michael?" She broke off crossly, for Michael had grasped her skirt in his hands and was shaking her.

"What is it, child?"

"Did she say she'd come back?" he cried, nearly knocking his Mother over. "Tell me – did she?"

Jane burst into tears.

"Mary Poppins is the only person I want in the world!" Michael wailed, and flung himself on to the floor.

"Really, children, really! I don't understand you. Do be good, I beg of you. There's nobody to look after you tonight. I have to go out to dinner and it's Ellen's Day Off. I shall have to send Mrs Brill up." And she kissed them absentmindedly, and went away with an anxious little line on her forehead . . .

"Well, if I ever did! Her going away and leaving you poor

dear children in the lurch like that," said Mrs Brill, a moment later, bustling in and setting to work on them.

"A heart of stone, that's what that girl had *and* no mistake, or my name's not Clara Brill. Always keeping herself to herself, too, and not even a lace handkerchief or a hatpin to remember her by. Get up, will you please, Master Michael!" Mrs Brill went on, panting heavily.

"How we stood her so long, I *don't* know – with her airs and graces and all. What a lot of buttons, Miss Jane! Stand still do now, and let me undress you, Master Michael. Plain she was, too, nothing much to look at. Indeed, all things considered, I don't know that we won't be better off, after all. Now, Miss Jane, where's your nightgown – why, what's this under your pillow—?"

Mrs Brill had drawn out a small knobbly parcel.

"What is it? Give it to me – give it," said Jane, trembling with excitement, and she took it from Mrs Brill's hands very quickly. Michael came and stood near her and watched her undo the string and tear away the brown paper. Mrs Brill, without waiting to see what emerged from the package, went in to the Twins.

The last wrapping fell to the floor and the thing that was in the parcel lay in Jane's hand.

"It's her picture,"

she said in a whisper, looking closely at it.

And it was!

Inside a little curly frame was a painting of Mary Poppins, and underneath it was written, "Mary Poppins by Bert".

"That's the Match Man – he did it," said Michael, and took it in his hand so that he could have a better look.

Jane found suddenly that there was a letter attached to the painting. She unfolded it carefully. It ran:

Dear Jane,

Michael had the compass
so the picture is for you.

Au revoir.

Mary Poppins

She read it out loud till she came to the words she couldn't understand.

"Mrs Brill!" she called. "What does '*au revoir*' mean?"

"Au revore, dearie?" shrieked Mrs Brill from the next room. "Why, doesn't it mean – let me see, I'm not up in these foreign tongues – doesn't it mean 'God bless you'? No. No, I'm wrong. I think, Miss Jane dear, it means 'To Meet Again'."

Jane and Michael looked at each other. Joy and understanding shone in their eyes. They knew what Mary Poppins meant.

Michael gave a long sigh of relief. "That's all right," he said shakily. "She always does what she says she will." He turned away.

"Michael, are you crying?" Jane asked.

He twisted his head and tried to smile at her.

"No, I am not," he said. "It is only my eyes."

She pushed him gently towards his bed, and as he got in she slipped the portrait of Mary Poppins into his hand – hurriedly, in case she should regret it.

"You have it for tonight, darling," whispered Jane, and she tucked him in just as Mary Poppins used to do . . .

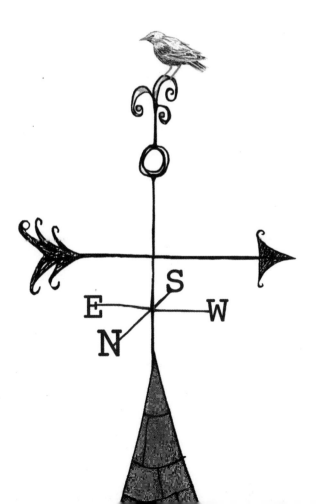

P. L. Travers

P. L. Travers was born in 1899, in Maryborough in Queensland, Australia, one of three sisters. She was a keen reader, particularly of all kinds of myths and legends, but before long she moved on to reading her mother's library books (which involved sneaking into her room while she was asleep!).

Pamela deliberately kept her life very private. She lived for a while in Ireland and London, and travelled frequently to America, where she was made writer in residence to both Smith and Radcliffe Colleges in Massachusetts. She also received an honorary doctorate from Chatham College, Pittsburgh.

Although she worked as a secretary, a dancer and an actress, writing was P. L. Travers's real love, and for many years she was a journalist. It was while she was recuperating from a serious illness that she wrote *Mary Poppins* – "to while away the days, but also to put down something that had been in my mind for a long time", she said. She received an OBE in 1977, and died in 1996.

Lauren Child

Lauren Child went to art school in London, and had a variety of jobs, as well as her own business designing lampshades, before becoming a children's-book creator. One of today's most innovative and highly regarded writers and artists, her books are loved the world over, winning multiple awards, including the acclaimed Kate Greenaway Medal. She is the renowned creator of the Charlie and Lola characters who appear in their own Bafta-winning television animation, as well as an accomplished novelist. Lauren is also the author of the bestselling Ruby Redfort series. She was named UNESCO's Artist for Peace in 2008 and awarded an MBE for services to literature in 2010. Passionate about the importance of quality books for children, Lauren is an ambassador for the National Literacy Trust, a trustee of the House of Illustration and was named Waterstones Children's Laureate in 2017.

A Note from the Illustrator

I'd very much like to thank Petit Pan, designers of wonderful fabric and haberdashery, for allowing me to use their prints as part of my illustration, and also Sara Fanelli for putting me in touch with them. Petit Pan's vivid colours and geometric patterns helped to bring a contemporary feel to this classic story.

Thanks also to Dashing Tweeds, who design innovative and beautiful tweed, for permission to include two of their eye-catching woven fabrics.

Lastly, thanks to Goldy Broad for her exquisite design.

Also by P. L. Travers

Publisher's Acknowledgements

A hallmark of Lauren Child's style of artwork is her distinct use of collage, fabric and cut-outs. The publishers would like to thank Petit Pan and Dashing Tweeds for their kind permission to reproduce the following fabrics in *Mary Poppins*.

Petit Pan® Paris   **DASHING TWEEDS**

BULLE NOIRE   CITRUS VERT   STELLA BLANC   BILLY GRIS   YELLOW RAVER

CHARDON ROUILLE   FRUITS BLEUS   HÉLIUM NOIR   PÉPIN BLEU   URBAN CYCLIST

www.petitpan.com   www.dashingtweeds.co.uk

First published in Great Britain by Peter Davies Ltd 1934
First published by HarperCollins 1958
This abridged edition published by HarperCollins *Children's Books* 2018
HarperCollins *Children's Books* is a division of HarperCollins*Publishers* Ltd,
1 London Bridge Street, London SE1 9GF

The HarperCollins website address is
www.harpercollins.co.uk

1 3 5 7 9 10 8 6 4 2

Text copyright reserved P. L. Travers 1934
Illustrations copyright © Lauren Child 2018

P. L. Travers and Lauren Child assert the moral right
to be identified as the author and illustrator of the work.

ISBN 978-0-00-828936-2

Printed and bound in Italy by
Rotolito S.p.A.

A CIP catalogue record for this book is available from the British Library.